For

Pamela

with love

Mom & Dad   12/04

DEAR DAUGHTER

With Love

Compiled by Suzanne Beilenson

Design by Lesley Ehlers

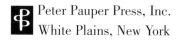 Peter Pauper Press, Inc.
White Plains, New York

Copyright © 1996
Peter Pauper Press, Inc.
202 Mamaroneck Avenue
White Plains, NY 10601
All rights reserved
ISBN 0-88088-112-7
Printed in Singapore
7 6 5 4 3 2 1

Contents

INTRODUCTION

You know you can always count on your mother. She's the first person you call when there's good news, and she's always there when you need a shoulder to cry on. And you can be sure that your mom will have some good advice if you need it. But just in case your mother can't be around, we've collected a cornucopia of quotes, letters, and wisdom from women and mothers around the world for you to turn to. We're sure you'll find them to be as smart, funny, and caring as your own mother.

S. B.

Love, Men, and Marriage

Dear Julie,

I sometimes think that falling in love is one of life's riskiest adventures—but what an adventure! Love is so exciting and so traumatic at the same time. Just remember that in any relationship you should stay as true to yourself as you do to the other person. In the midst of love, it's easy to lose sight of yourself and what's important to you. You really have to work at it. When you love and accept yourself, you have much more to offer.

Love,

Mom

To keep the fire burning brightly there's one
easy rule: Keep the two logs together, near
enough to keep each other warm and far enough
apart—about a finger's breadth—for breathing
room. Good fire, good marriage, same rule.

Marnie Reed Crowell

So long as a woman is dependent on a man for
her self-image or her self-esteem she will remain
without any sense of her own worth—can never
be a fully realized human being.

Eleanor Perry

The test of a happily married—and a wise—
woman is whether she can say, "I love you" far
oftener than she asks, "Do you love me?"

Dorothy Dayton

𝒯he only time a woman really succeeds in changing a man is when he's a baby.

Natalie Wood

❦

𝒢etting along with men isn't what's truly important. The vital knowledge is how to get along with a man, one man.

Phyllis McGinley

❦

𝒜s the rolling stone gathers no moss, so the roving heart gathers no affections.

Mrs. Jameson

❦

One puzzling thing about men—they allow their sex instinct to drive them to where their intelligence never would take them.

Joan Fontaine

Don't love everybody—specialize.

Anonymous parent

Make sure you never, never argue at night. You just lose a good night's sleep, and you can't settle anything until morning anyway.

Rose Kennedy

$\mathcal{L}$ove . . . is the extremely difficult realization
that something other than oneself is real.

Iris Murdoch

$\mathcal{A}$ woman's lot is made for her by the love she
accepts.

George Eliot

$\mathcal{L}$ove is the vital essence that pervades and per-
meates, from the center to the circumference, the
graduating circles of all thought and action. Love
is the talisman of human weal and woe—the
open sesame to every human soul.

Elizabeth Cady Stanton

Marriage is not just spiritual communion and passionate embraces; marriage is also three-meals-a-day and remembering to carry out the trash.

Joyce Brothers

A broken heart is what makes life so wonderful five years later, when you see the guy in an elevator and he is fat and smoking a cigar and saying long-time-no-see.

Phyllis Battelle

In those days, it didn't matter: you could be a Wimbledon champion, Phi Beta Kappa, Miss America, Nobel Peace Prize winner, but if they asked you about marriage and you didn't at least have a hot prospect ready to get down on one knee, you knew you were considered to be no more than half a woman.

Billie Jean King

Every man is a volume if you know how to read him.

Margaret Fuller

Love is moral even without legal marriage, but marriage is immoral without love.

Ellen Key

Any one must see at a glance that if men and women marry those whom they do not love, they must love those whom they do not marry.

Harriet Martineau

Trust your husband, adore your husband, and get as much as you can in your own name.

Advice to Joan Rivers from her mother

Age does not protect you from love. But love, to some extent, protects you from age.

Jeanne Moreau

So many persons think divorce a panacea for every ill, find out, when they try it, that the remedy is worse than the disease.

Dorothy Dix

Trouble is a part of your life, and if you don't share it, you don't give the person who loves you a chance to love you enough.

Dinah Shore

Chains do not hold a marriage together. It is threads, hundreds of tiny threads which sew people together through the years. That's what makes a marriage last—more than passion or even sex.

Simone Signoret

$\mathcal{L}$ook for a sweet person. Forget rich.

Estée Lauder

$\mathcal{M}$arriage—A book of which the first chapter is written in poetry and the remaining chapters in prose.

Beverley Nichols

$\mathcal{A}$ll women know the value of love. But few will pay the price.

Beth Ellis

$\mathcal{M}$y ancestors wandered lost in the wilderness for 40 years because even in biblical times, men would not stop to ask for directions.

Elayne Boosler

$\mathcal{L}$ove is like playing checkers. You have to know which man to move.

Jackie "Moms" Mabley

$\mathcal{M}$arriage involves big compromises all the time. International-level compromises. You're the U.S.A., he's the USSR, and you're talking nuclear warheads.

Bette Midler

$\mathcal{L}$ove makes mutes of those who habitually speak most fluently.

Madeleine de Scudéry

$\mathcal{I}$t is easier to keep half a dozen lovers guessing than to keep one lover after he has stopped guessing.

Helen Rowland

$\mathcal{F}$ree love is sometimes love but never freedom.

Elizabeth Bibesco

Age and Beauty

Dear Marjorie,

When I saw you last night, I realized what a beautiful woman you had become. It wasn't just the dress
or your hair, but something inside of you was radiant
too. All of your warmth and dedication and love
came shining through. Whoever said beauty was only
skin deep never saw you, my lovely daughter. You
have true inner beauty, the kind that comes from
caring passionately about the people in your life and
from cultivating your mind as well as your body.
And, in the future, there will never be a grey hair or
wrinkle that could take away from your beauty—
because it comes from within.

Love always,

Mom

*B*eauty, what is that? . . . Beauty neither buys
food nor keeps up a home.

Maxine Elliott

*B*eautiful young people are accidents of
nature. But beautiful old people are works of art.

Marjorie Barstow Greenbie

A woman past forty should make up her mind
to be young—not her face.

Billie Burke

$\mathcal{I}$m tired of all this nonsense about beauty
being only skin-deep. That's deep enough. What
do you want—an adorable pancreas?

Jean Kerr

$\mathcal{Y}$ou can take no credit for beauty at sixteen.
But if you are beautiful at sixty, it will be your
own soul's doing.

Marie Carmichael Stopes

$\mathcal{B}$eauty is in the eye of the beholder.

Margaret W. Hungerford

There is no cosmetic for beauty like happiness.

Lady Marguerite Blessington

There are three things a woman ought to look—
straight as a dart, supple as a snake, and proud
as a tiger lily.

Elinor Glyn

Yet this is health: To have a body functioning
so perfectly that when its few simple needs are
met it never calls attention to its own existence.
. . . If the machine is going to work over a long
period of time at maximum efficiency, it must
receive intelligent care.

Bertha Stuart Dyment

There are no ugly women, only lazy ones.

Helena Rubinstein

Circumstances alter faces.

Carolyn Wells

One of the few advantages to not being beautiful is that one usually gets better-looking as one gets older; I am, in fact, at this very moment gaining my looks.

Nora Ephron

Character contributes to beauty. It fortifies a woman as her youth fades. A mode of conduct, a standard of courage, discipline, fortitude and integrity can do a great deal to make a woman beautiful.

Jacqueline Bisset

Strength of body, and that character of countenance which the French term a physionomie, women do not acquire before thirty, any more than men.

Mary Wollstonecraft

The beauty that addresses itself to the eyes is only the spell of the moment; the eye of the body is not always that of the soul.

George Sand

These are very confusing times. For the first time in history a woman is expected to combine: intelligence with a sharp hairdo, a raised consciousness with high heels, and an open, non-sexist relationship with a tan guy who has a great bod.

Lynda Barry

$\mathcal{L}$ife does not count by years. Some suffer a life-time in a day, and so grow old between the rising and the setting of the sun.

Augusta Jane Evans

$\mathcal{T}$here is new strength, repose of mind, and inspiration in fresh apparel.

Ella Wheeler Wilcox

$\mathcal{Y}$ou're never too old to become younger.

Mae West

$\mathcal{B}$eauty is not caused. It is.

Emily Dickinson

Work, Success,
Money

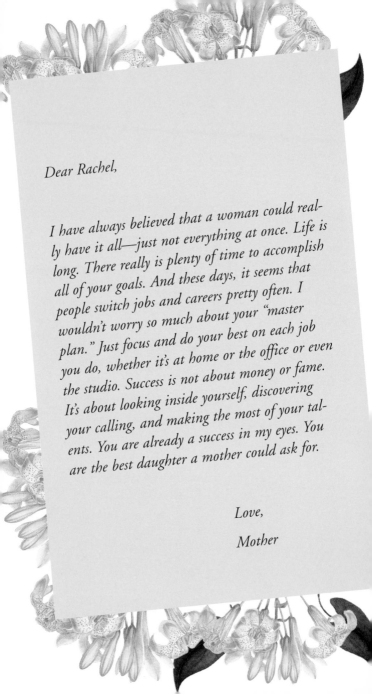

Dear Rachel,

I have always believed that a woman could really have it all—just not everything at once. Life is long. There really is plenty of time to accomplish all of your goals. And these days, it seems that people switch jobs and careers pretty often. I wouldn't worry so much about your "master plan." Just focus and do your best on each job you do, whether it's at home or the office or even the studio. Success is not about money or fame. It's about looking inside yourself, discovering your calling, and making the most of your talents. You are already a success in my eyes. You are the best daughter a mother could ask for.

Love,

Mother

The secret of joy in work is contained in one word—excellence. To know how to do something well is to enjoy it.

Pearl Buck

The best careers advice given to the young is "Find out what you like doing best and get someone to pay you for doing it."

Katharine Whitehorn

Don't be afraid to start at the bottom.

Phyllis Grann

$\mathscr{A}$ woman has to be twice as good as a man to go half as far.

Fannie Hurst

$\mathscr{P}$ower is your ability to be a leader and get people to follow.

Sandra Kurtzig

$\mathscr{T}$he easiest way for your children to learn about money is for you not to have any.

Katharine Whitehorn

When you earn it and spend it you do know the difference between three dollars and a million dollars, but when you say it and vote it, it all sounds the same.

Gertrude Stein

If people think you are immersed, are serious and have done your homework, then they take you seriously.

Carla Hills

Wealth is something you acquire so you can share it, not keep it.

LaDonna Harris

$\mathcal{M}$oney never remains just coins and pieces of paper. It is constantly changing into the comforts of daily life. Money can be translated into the beauty of living, a support in misfortune, an education, or future security. It also can be translated into a source of bitterness.

Sylvia Porter

$\mathcal{B}$ut it is my firm belief that the main source of happiness in life is work. Whatsoever that work may be, I have found that the best gift life can give us is that we have something to set our hand to, something in which to be busy, in which we may be productive.

Kirsten Flagstad

$\mathcal{W}$hat one has to do usually can be done.

Eleanor Roosevelt

To love what you do and feel that it matters—
how could anything be more fun?

Katharine Graham

To be successful, a woman has to be much better at her job than a man.

Golda Meir

The experience taught me that you don't have to
put up with nasty bosses or do things you don't
agree with. If you believe in yourself and work
hard, you can always find another job. That feel-
ing helped me start my own business three years
later, and gave me the confidence that I could
make it a success.

Eileen Ford

There's a real fulfillment when you use your talent to help make the world a better place.

Barbra Streisand

_I_ think self-awareness is probably the most important thing towards being a champion.

Billie Jean King

_If_ you want to succeed in the world it is necessary, when entering a salon, that your vanity should bow to that of others.

Madame de Genlis

$\mathscr{F}$igure out what your most magnificent qualities
are and make them indispensable to the people
you want to work with. Notice that I didn't say
"work for."

Linda Bloodworth-Thomason

$\mathscr{A}$ girl should not expect special privileges
because of her sex, but neither should she
"adjust" to prejudice and discrimination. She
must learn to compete then, not as a woman, but
as a human being.

Betty Friedan

*I*f you really want something, you can figure out how to make it happen.

Cher

*E*veryone has talent. What is rare is the courage to follow the talent to the dark place where it leads.

Erica Jong

*H*ouse-keeping ain't no joke.

Louisa May Alcott,
Little Women

*M*oney, like manure, should be spread around.

Brooke Astor

*I*t's very important to define success for yourself. If you really want to reach for the brass
ring, just remember that there are sacrifices that
go along.

Cathleen Black

*W*omen are never stronger than when they arm
themselves with their weaknesses.

Madame du Deffand

$\mathcal{L}$ack of will power has caused more failure than lack of intelligence or ability.

Flower A. Newhouse

$\mathcal{T}$otal commitment to family and total commitment to career is possible, but fatiguing.

Muriel Fox

$\mathcal{I}$f you can't give money, give of yourself. Giving will make you strong and happy.

Brooke Astor

*Live and
Be Happy*

Dear Lisa,

What a fragile, wispy creature Happiness is. Just when you think you have it all wrapped up, something seems to upset the whole balance. That's life, though. Ups and Downs. Keeping perspective is the key. If you worry too much about the bumps in the road, you'll miss all the scenery. So, slow down. Enjoy the view. And if every now and then you don't like the path you're traveling, remember there's always another route you can take. Or even better, stop by and see me—Exit 15 off the parkway!

Keep on truckin'

Your Mom

Happiness is not a state to arrive at, but a manner of traveling.

Margaret Lee Runbeck

Happiness is not perfected until it is shared.

Jane Porter

Yesterday is a canceled check; tomorrow is a promissory note; today is ready cash—use it.

Kay Lyons

It costs a great deal to be reasonable; it costs youth.

Madame de La Fayette

We grow neither better nor worse as we get old,
but more like ourselves.

May Lamberton Becker

To possess character is to be useful, and to be
useful is to be independent, and to be useful and
independent is to be happy, even in the midst of
sorrow; for sorrow is not necessarily unhappi-
ness.

Ella Wheeler Wilcox

If only we'd stop trying to be happy we could
have a pretty good time.

Edith Wharton

$\mathcal{N}$o one grows old by living—only by losing interest in living.

Marie Ray

Live as if you expected to live an hundred years, but might die to-morrow.

Ann Lee

Keep breathing.

Sophie Tucker,
advice on how to live a long life

$\mathcal{T}$he only way to enjoy anything in this life is to earn it first.

Ginger Rogers

$\mathcal{M}$y mother, who is my spiritual touchstone, told me to remember three things in life: "You have one body, respect it; one mind, feed it well; and one life—enjoy it."

Des'ree

$\mathcal{T}$he richness of our own lives, creative and receptive, depends on how closely we identify ourselves with the struggles and problems, individual and social, as well as with the hopes and ideals of the age in which we live.

Anita Block

$\mathscr{A}$ge is not measured by years. Nature does not equally distribute energy. Some people are born old and tired while others are going strong at 70.

Dorothy Thompson

$\mathscr{T}$he trick is not how much pain you feel—but how much joy you feel. Any idiot can feel pain. Life is full of excuses to feel pain, excuses not to live, excuses, excuses, excuses.

Erica Jong

$\mathscr{Y}$ou had better live your best and act your best and think your best today; for today is the sure preparation for tomorrow and all the other tomorrows that follow.

Harriet Martineau

A Mother's
Wisdom

Dear Barbara,

When I think of all the things I've learned so far in my life—from mistakes, from good decisions, and even from dumb luck, all I want to do is to pass it on to you. Experience is an awfully good teacher. So bear with me when I seem to be trying to tell you what to do. I want so much for you to be happy, and to help you avoid some of life's pitfalls. I know when Grandma would pass on advice to me, it sometimes made me crazy. Every now and then, though, something she told me made all the difference. Maybe Mother does know best— most of the time!

Love,

Mom

$\mathcal{F}$ollow your instincts. That's where true wisdom manifests itself.

Oprah Winfrey

$\mathcal{W}$e must not, in trying to think about how we can make a big difference, ignore the small daily differences we can make which, over time, add up to big differences that we often cannot foresee.

Marian Wright Edelman

$\mathcal{N}$othing in life is to be feared. It is only to be understood.

Marie Curie

*N*ever grow a wishbone, daughter, where your backbone ought to be.

Clementine Paddleford

❦

*F*riendship with oneself is all-important, because without it one cannot be friends with anyone else in the world.

Eleanor Roosevelt

❦

A first failure is often a blessing.

Antoinette L. Brown

❦

There are two ways of meeting difficulties: you alter the difficulties, or you alter yourself to meet them.

Phyllis Bottome

There's one thing to be said for inviting trouble: it generally accepts.

Mae Maloo

On the human chessboard, all moves are possible.

Miriam Schiff

The distance is nothing; it is only the first step that is difficult.

Madame du Deffand

There's always room for improvement—it's the biggest room in the house.

Louise Heath Leber

Do not rely completely on any other human being, however dear. We meet all life's greatest tests alone.

Agnes Macphail

$\mathcal{W}$e have to work to be good people, . . . goodness always involves the choice to be good.

Liv Ullmann

$\mathcal{I}$ know my daughter will someday see her own mother with kinder eyes. But in less sane times, when I am flushed with years and my daughter is mortified by my very being, I am apt to forget all this and take her current feelings—my own feelings at her age—as fixed for the rest of my days.

S. Holly Stocking

$\mathcal{T}$he thing you have to be prepared for is that other people don't always dream your dream.

Linda Ronstadt

Don't call it loneliness. Call it something else. Call it solitude. I don't mean to be glib, but if you're not good company for yourself, you have to work to become the kind of person whose company you enjoy. If you enjoy your own company, there is no loneliness.

Toni Morrison

When somebody says to me—which they do like every five years—"How does it feel to be over the hill," my response is, "I'm just heading up the mountain."

Joan Baez

$\mathcal{O}$ur friendships are the currency of our lives. They may be the only currency of our lives. In the absence of so many support systems, we are it for each other.

Toni Morrison

❦

$\mathcal{Y}$ou are what you are when nobody is looking.

Abigail Van Buren and Ann Landers

❦

$\mathcal{C}$haracter building begins in our infancy and continues until death.

Eleanor Roosevelt

❦

*I*f you rest, you rust.

Helen Hayes

A really interesting life has embraced everything from the most magnificent exultation to the
depths of tragedy. I would say that's tremendous
expérience. But I wouldn't say enjoyment is an
accurate summary of it.

Marcia Davenport

*W*ho knows what women can be when they are
finally free to become themselves.

Betty Friedan

To live exhilaratingly in and for the moment is deadly serious work, fun of the most exhausting sort.

Barbara Grizzuti Harrison

Perhaps one has to be very old before one learns how to be amused rather than shocked.

Pearl Buck

Don't compromise yourself. You are all you've got.

Janis Joplin

Experience is a good teacher, but she sends in terrific bills.

Minna Antrim

A happy woman is one who has no cares at all; a cheerful woman is one who has cares but doesn't let them get her down.

Beverly Sills

There are three ways to get something done: do it yourself, hire someone, or forbid your kids to do it.

Monta Crane